Picking
Pickle

WELCOME
please wipe your feet!

STERLING CHILDREN'S BOOKS
New York

This book has
been adopted by

....

who will give it a
loving home forever

For Bill and Eddie, with love PF
For Fay and Trevor, with love CV

STERLING CHILDREN'S BOOKS
New York

An Imprint of Sterling Publishing Co., Inc.
1166 Avenue of the Americas
New York, NY 10036

Text © 2018 Polly Faber
illustrations © 2018 Clara Vulliamy

First published in the United Kingdom in 2018 by Pavilion Children's Books, 43 Great Ormond St, London, WC1N 3HZ

ISBN 978-1-4549-3295-6

Distributed in Canada by Sterling Publishing c/o Canadian Manda Group, 664 Annette Street Toronto, Ontario M6S 2C8, Canada

For information about custom editions, special sales, and premium and corporate purchases, please contact Sterling Special Sales at 800-805-5489 or specialsales@sterlingpublishing.com.

Manufactured in China
Lot #:
2 4 6 8 10 9 7 5 3 1
09/18

sterlingpublishing.com

Picking
Pickle

by Polly Faber & Clara Vulliamy

Hello!

Have *you* come to choose a dog?

How exciting!

Picking can be tricky though.

Can I help?

I've been here the longest.

I know *everyone*.

I'll find the perfect
match for you.
Let me sniff...

...mmmm—you smell *great*.

Come and meet

Geraldo.

He's *very* handsome.

He's won prizes:

rosettes and a silver cup.

BEST IN
SHOW

He enjoys a stroke
of those silky ears—
go on!

Best
Dog
1st Prize

1

Smoothest
Coat
1st Prize

1

But *are* those his ears or...

the other end?

Silkiest
Ears
1st Prize

You wouldn't want to get it wrong.

How about

HARVEY?

We all

look up

to Harvey.

He's got quite an appetite.

Did I smell *treats* in your pocket?

Harvey may have smelled them, too.

You might need
to give him one.

Or two...

or three... or

HARVEY!

And here is **Dumpling.**

She's *ever* so smart.

She chews through news,
opinions, *and* the crossword
in seconds.

She speaks five different languages!

Hello!

Guten tag!

你好!

Hola!

Bonjour!

All at the same time!

But I haven't asked...

...what do you need your dog to do?

If you're after a guard or

a working animal you'll find

Matilda

has *excellent* teeth.

WIGGINS

is *very* good at...

HOOOWL!

loudness!

And Dibble

can round up *anything!*

You brought a ball? My favorite!

Can I bring it back?

Can I bring it back again?

Can I bring it
back *again*?

For sporty fun you must meet

BOo-BoO!

Boo-Boo almost *is* a ball, he's so bouncy.

He is *fast*.

Have a rest.

This is harder
than usual.

A tummy rub for me?
Why thank you! I *love* them.

Ahhh...

You deserve the best of all.
And the *best* dog here is *definitely*...

Poochy Petunia Wuffles - Winstanley

You can see she has breeding.

Look at her nose!

Look at her certificate in a frame!

She is waiting for someone perfect.

Someone like you.

Small questions:

Can you offer a golden bowl?

A diamond collar?

Dinner with royalty every week?

Now *that* isn't good behavior.
I'm so sorry.

I don't know what to say.
I can't understand it.

Is there no dog
here that's right?
This *is* a pickle.

What's that?

You *have* chosen? You know *exactly* who you want to take home forever?

Oh.

That's... good news.

Very good news.

I'm happy for them.

Tell me, please.

Who is it to be?